BEYOND ™

VOLUME 12: BATTLE OF THE MONSTERS

Written by	Illustrated by
R.L. Stine	**Kelly & Nichole Matthews**

Lettered by	Cover by	*Just Beyond* created by
Mike Fiorentino	**Miguel Mercado**	**R.L. Stine**

Designer	Associate Editor	Editor
Scott Newman	**Sophie Philips-Roberts**	**Bryce Carlson**

ABDOBOOKS.COM

Reinforced library bound edition published in 2022 by Spotlight, a division of ABDO, PO Box 398166, Minneapolis, Minnesota 55439. Spotlight produces high-quality reinforced library bound editions for schools and libraries. Published by agreement with KaBOOM!

Printed in the United States of America, North Mankato, Minnesota.
042021   092021

Library of Congress Control Number: 2020949741

Publisher's Cataloging-in-Publication Data

Names: Stine, R.L., author. | Matthews, Kelly; Matthews, Nichole, illustrators.
Title: Battle of the monsters / by R.L. Stine ; illustrated by Kelly Matthews and Nichole Matthews.
Description: Minneapolis, Minnesota : Spotlight, 2022. | Series: Just beyond; volume 12
Summary: The friendlier village turns out to be a prison where Koroko stores his food, and the group has to figure out how to free the prisoners and how to escape from Beast Island.
Identifiers: ISBN 9781532148316 (lib. bdg.)
Subjects: LCSH: Brothers and sisters--Juvenile fiction. | Prisons--Juvenile fiction. | Escapes--Juvenile fiction. | Ghost stories--Juvenile fiction. | Middle school students--Juvenile fiction. | Graphic novels--Juvenile fiction.
Classification: DDC 741.5--dc23

Spotlight
A Division of ABDO
abdobooks.com

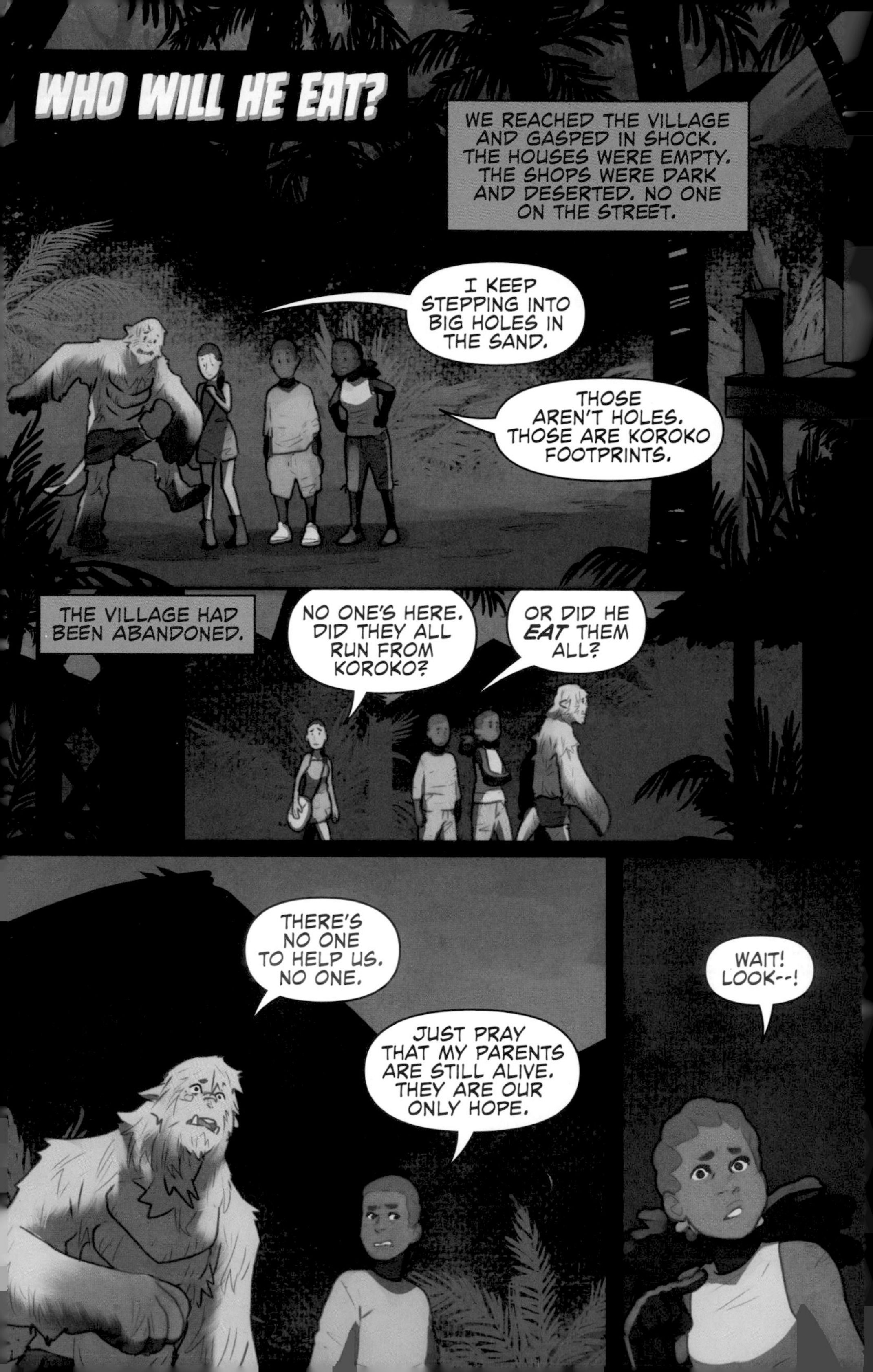
WHO WILL HE EAT?
WE REACHED THE VILLAGE AND GASPED IN SHOCK. THE HOUSES WERE EMPTY. THE SHOPS WERE DARK AND DESERTED. NO ONE ON THE STREET.
I KEEP STEPPING INTO BIG HOLES IN THE SAND.
THOSE AREN'T HOLES. THOSE ARE KOROKO FOOTPRINTS.
THE VILLAGE HAD BEEN ABANDONED.
NO ONE'S HERE. DID THEY ALL RUN FROM KOROKO?
OR DID HE EAT THEM ALL?
THERE'S NO ONE TO HELP US. NO ONE.
JUST PRAY THAT MY PARENTS ARE STILL ALIVE. THEY ARE OUR ONLY HOPE.
WAIT! LOOK--!

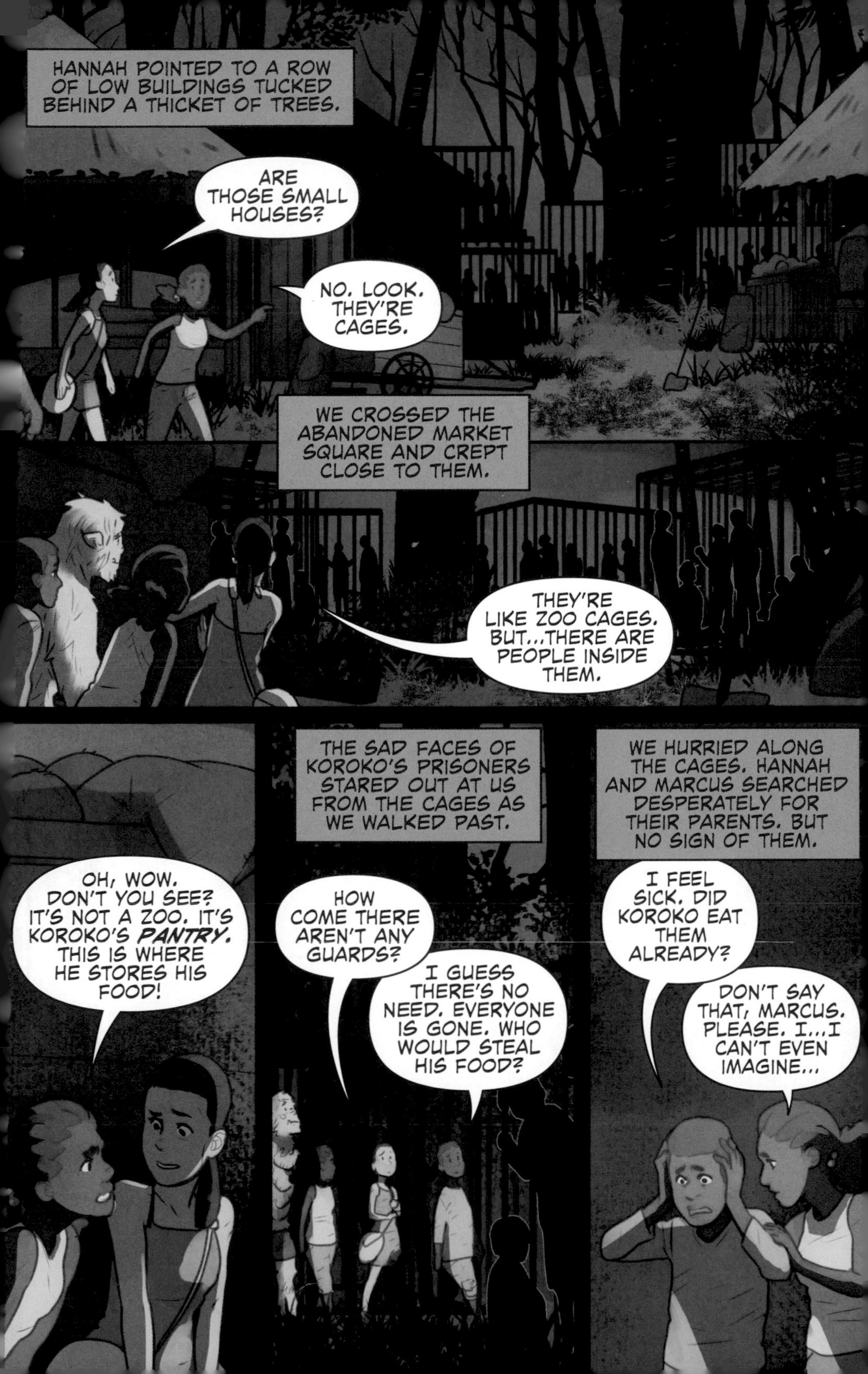
HANNAH POINTED TO A ROW OF LOW BUILDINGS TUCKED BEHIND A THICKET OF TREES.
ARE THOSE SMALL HOUSES?
NO. LOOK. THEY'RE CAGES.
WE CROSSED THE ABANDONED MARKET SQUARE AND CREPT CLOSE TO THEM.
THEY'RE LIKE ZOO CAGES. BUT...THERE ARE PEOPLE INSIDE THEM.
OH, WOW. DON'T YOU SEE? IT'S NOT A ZOO. IT'S KOROKO'S *PANTRY*. THIS IS WHERE HE STORES HIS FOOD!
THE SAD FACES OF KOROKO'S PRISONERS STARED OUT AT US FROM THE CAGES AS WE WALKED PAST.
HOW COME THERE AREN'T ANY GUARDS?
I GUESS THERE'S NO NEED. EVERYONE IS GONE. WHO WOULD STEAL HIS FOOD?
WE HURRIED ALONG THE CAGES. HANNAH AND MARCUS SEARCHED DESPERATELY FOR THEIR PARENTS. BUT NO SIGN OF THEM.
I FEEL SICK. DID KOROKO EAT THEM ALREADY?
DON'T SAY THAT, MARCUS. PLEASE. I...I CAN'T EVEN IMAGINE...

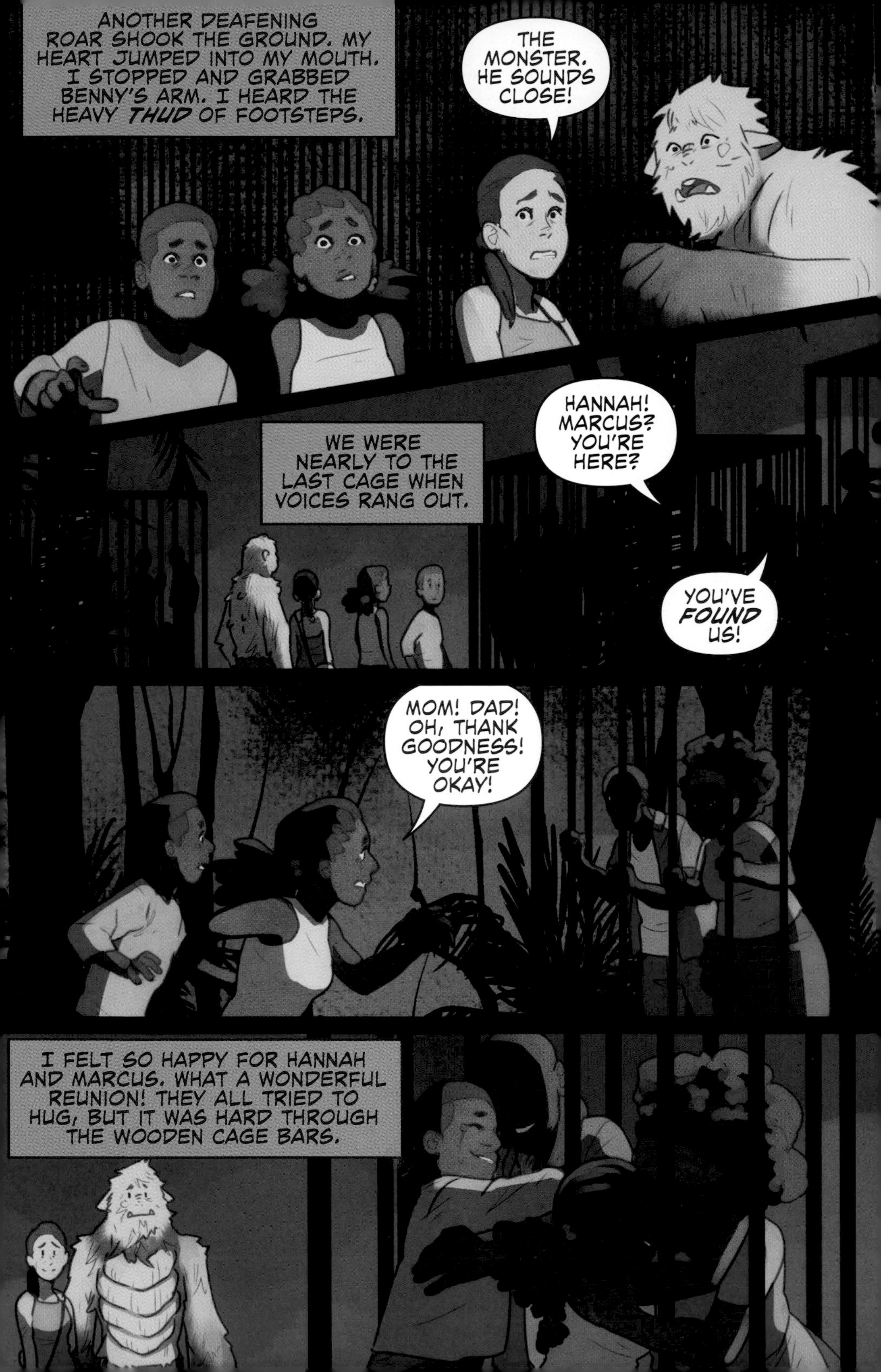
ANOTHER DEAFENING ROAR SHOOK THE GROUND. MY HEART JUMPED INTO MY MOUTH. I STOPPED AND GRABBED BENNY'S ARM. I HEARD THE HEAVY *THUD* OF FOOTSTEPS.
THE MONSTER. HE SOUNDS CLOSE!
WE WERE NEARLY TO THE LAST CAGE WHEN VOICES RANG OUT.
HANNAH! MARCUS? YOU'RE HERE?
YOU'VE *FOUND* US!
MOM! DAD! OH, THANK GOODNESS! YOU'RE OKAY!
I FELT SO HAPPY FOR HANNAH AND MARCUS. WHAT A WONDERFUL REUNION! THEY ALL TRIED TO HUG, BUT IT WAS HARD THROUGH THE WOODEN CAGE BARS.

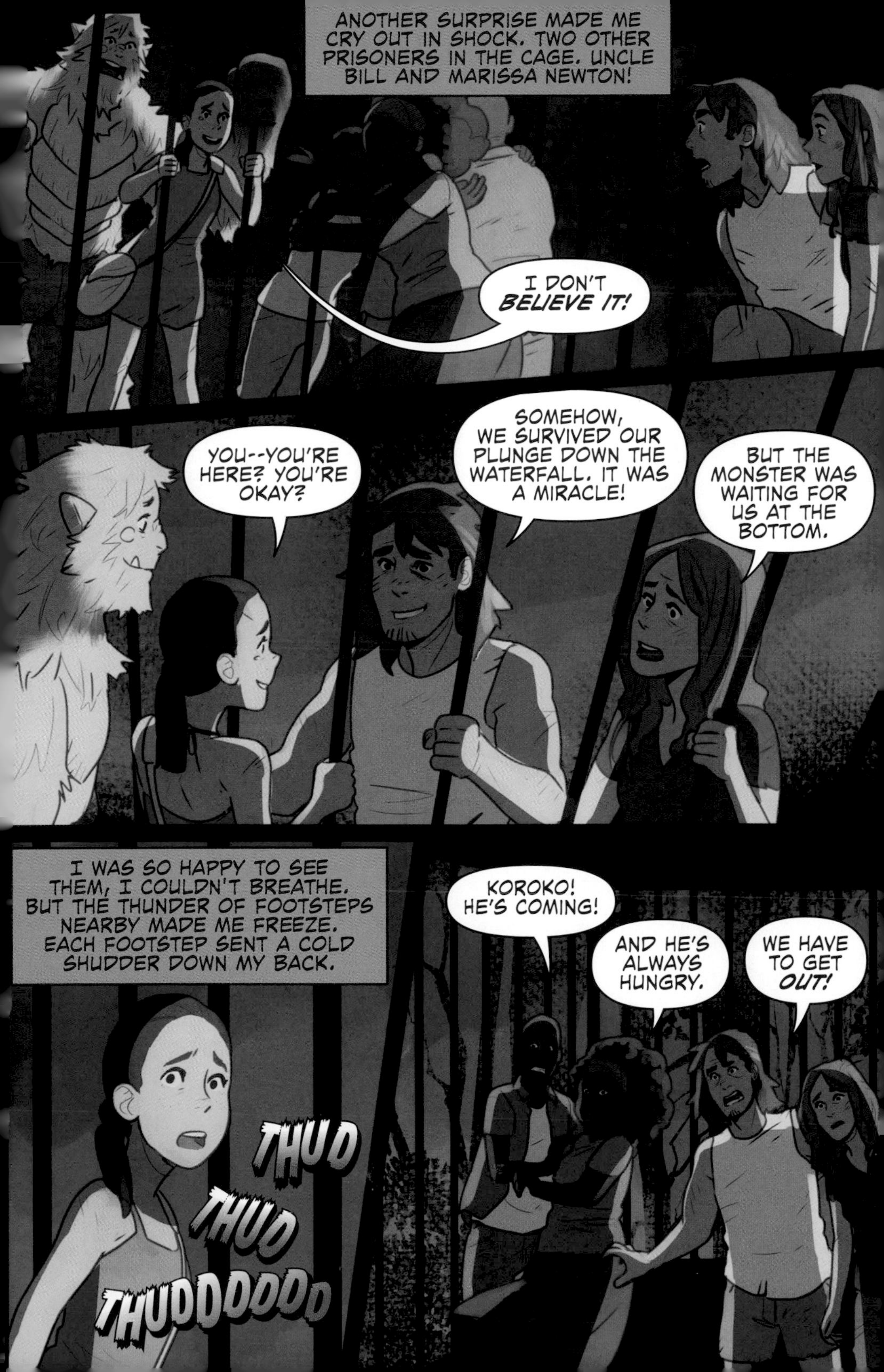
ANOTHER SURPRISE MADE ME CRY OUT IN SHOCK. TWO OTHER PRISONERS IN THE CAGE. UNCLE BILL AND MARISSA NEWTON!
I DON'T BELIEVE IT!
YOU--YOU'RE HERE? YOU'RE OKAY?
SOMEHOW, WE SURVIVED OUR PLUNGE DOWN THE WATERFALL. IT WAS A MIRACLE!
BUT THE MONSTER WAS WAITING FOR US AT THE BOTTOM.
I WAS SO HAPPY TO SEE THEM, I COULDN'T BREATHE. BUT THE THUNDER OF FOOTSTEPS NEARBY MADE ME FREEZE. EACH FOOTSTEP SENT A COLD SHUDDER DOWN MY BACK.
THUD
THUD
THUDDDDDD
KOROKO! HE'S COMING!
AND HE'S ALWAYS HUNGRY.
WE HAVE TO GET OUT!

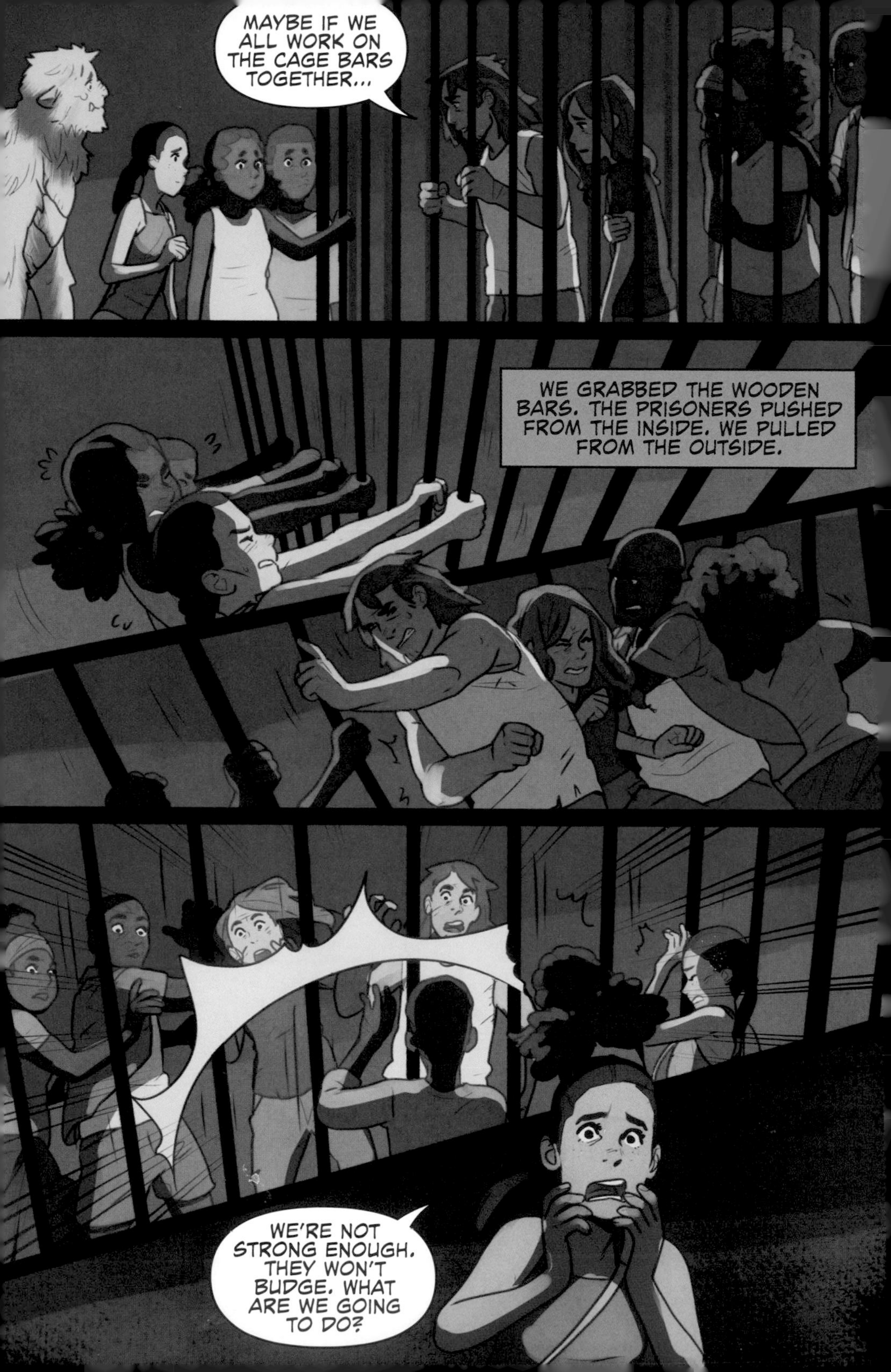
MAYBE IF WE ALL WORK ON THE CAGE BARS TOGETHER...
WE GRABBED THE WOODEN BARS. THE PRISONERS PUSHED FROM THE INSIDE. WE PULLED FROM THE OUTSIDE.
WE'RE NOT STRONG ENOUGH. THEY WON'T BUDGE. WHAT ARE WE GOING TO DO?

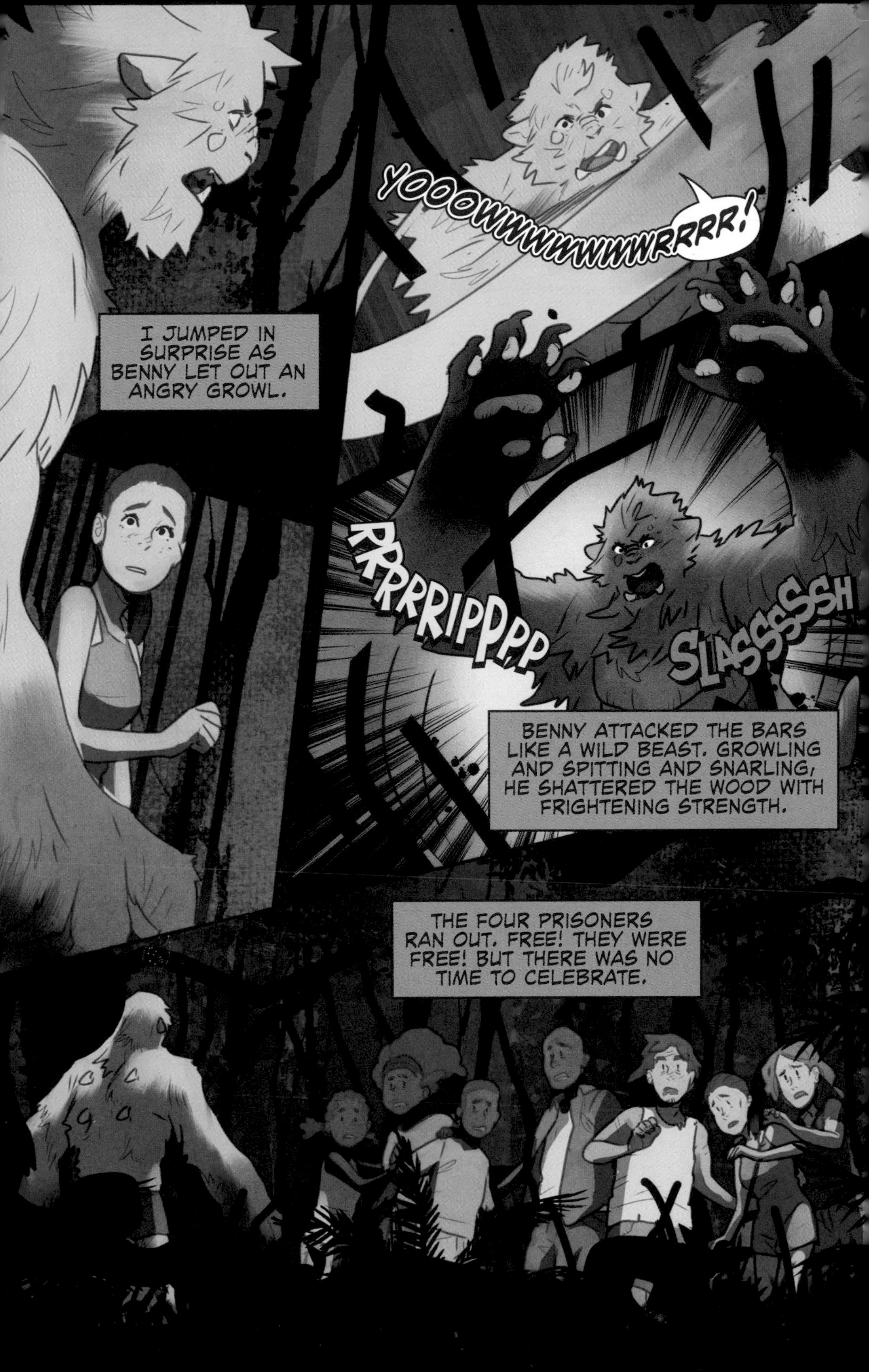
YOOOWWWWWWWWRRRR!
I JUMPED IN SURPRISE AS BENNY LET OUT AN ANGRY GROWL.
RRRRRIPPPPP
SLASSSSSSH
BENNY ATTACKED THE BARS LIKE A WILD BEAST. GROWLING AND SPITTING AND SNARLING, HE SHATTERED THE WOOD WITH FRIGHTENING STRENGTH.
THE FOUR PRISONERS RAN OUT. FREE! THEY WERE FREE! BUT THERE WAS NO TIME TO CELEBRATE.

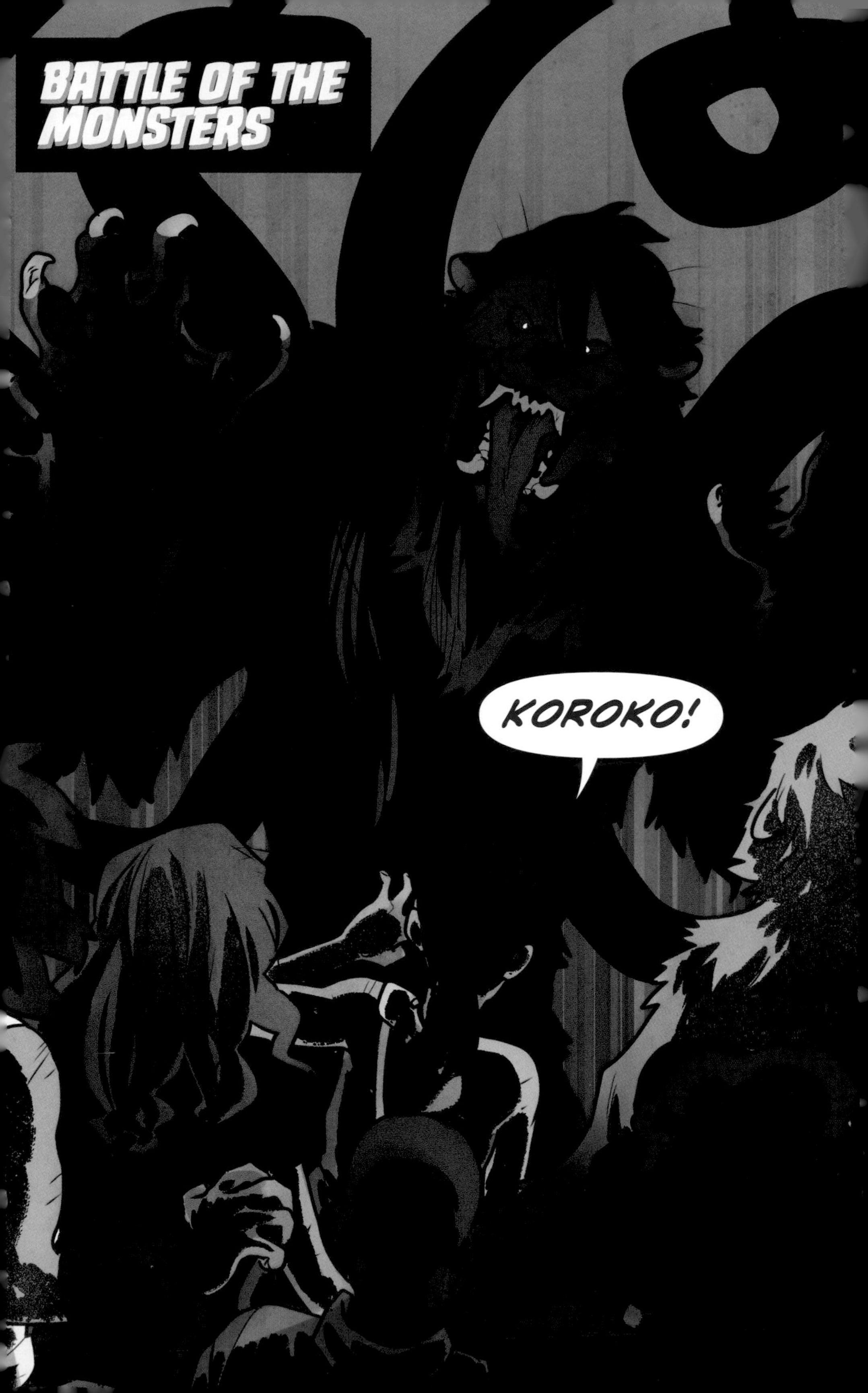
BATTLE OF THE MONSTERS
KOROKO!

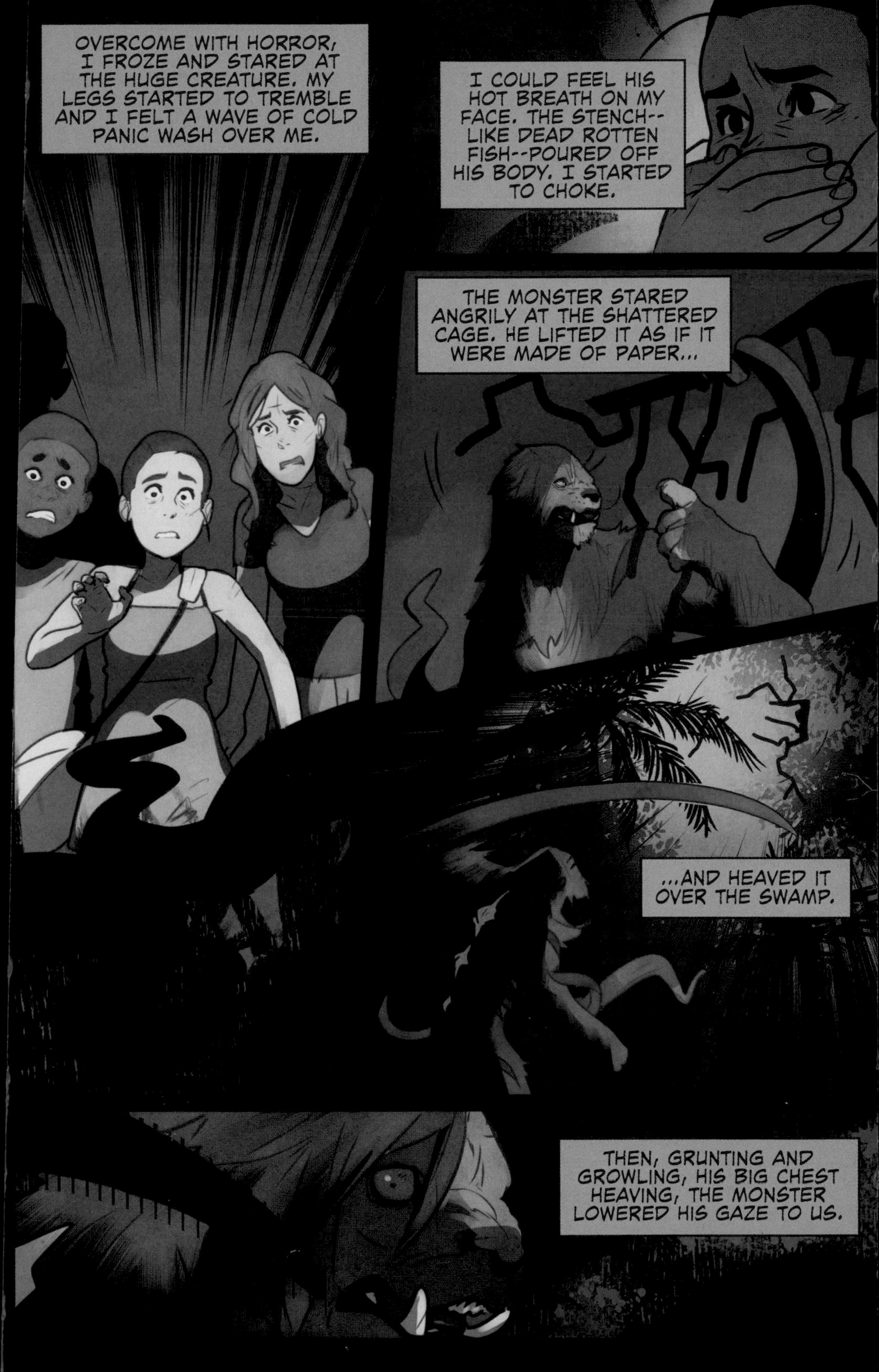
OVERCOME WITH HORROR, I FROZE AND STARED AT THE HUGE CREATURE. MY LEGS STARTED TO TREMBLE AND I FELT A WAVE OF COLD PANIC WASH OVER ME.
I COULD FEEL HIS HOT BREATH ON MY FACE. THE STENCH--LIKE DEAD ROTTEN FISH--POURED OFF HIS BODY. I STARTED TO CHOKE.
THE MONSTER STARED ANGRILY AT THE SHATTERED CAGE. HE LIFTED IT AS IF IT WERE MADE OF PAPER...
...AND HEAVED IT OVER THE SWAMP.
THEN, GRUNTING AND GROWLING, HIS BIG CHEST HEAVING, THE MONSTER LOWERED HIS GAZE TO US.

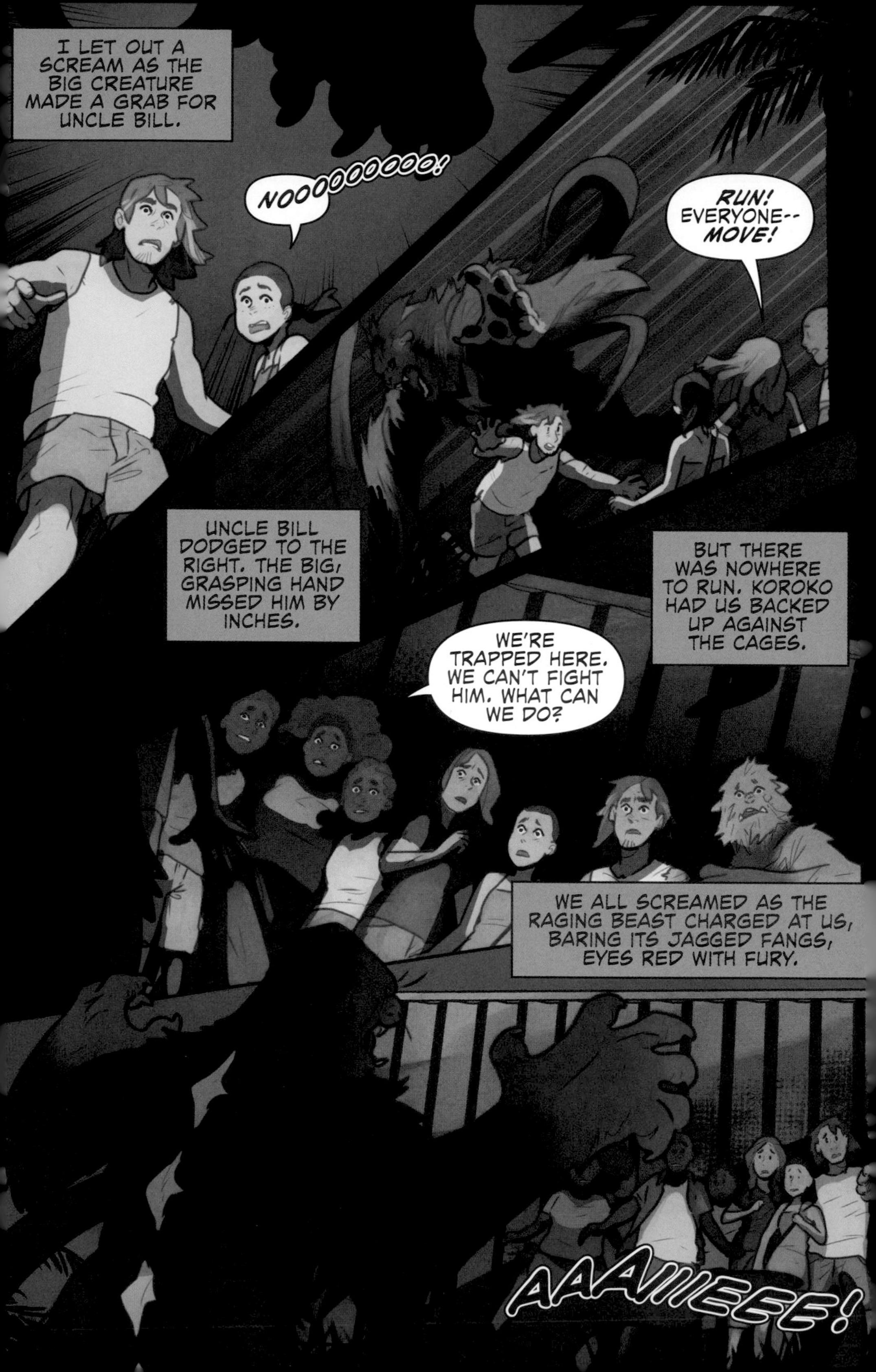
I LET OUT A SCREAM AS THE BIG CREATURE MADE A GRAB FOR UNCLE BILL.
NOOOOOOOOO!
RUN! EVERYONE-- MOVE!
UNCLE BILL DODGED TO THE RIGHT. THE BIG, GRASPING HAND MISSED HIM BY INCHES.
BUT THERE WAS NOWHERE TO RUN. KOROKO HAD US BACKED UP AGAINST THE CAGES.
WE'RE TRAPPED HERE. WE CAN'T FIGHT HIM. WHAT CAN WE DO?
WE ALL SCREAMED AS THE RAGING BEAST CHARGED AT US, BARING ITS JAGGED FANGS, EYES RED WITH FURY.
AAAIIIEEEE!

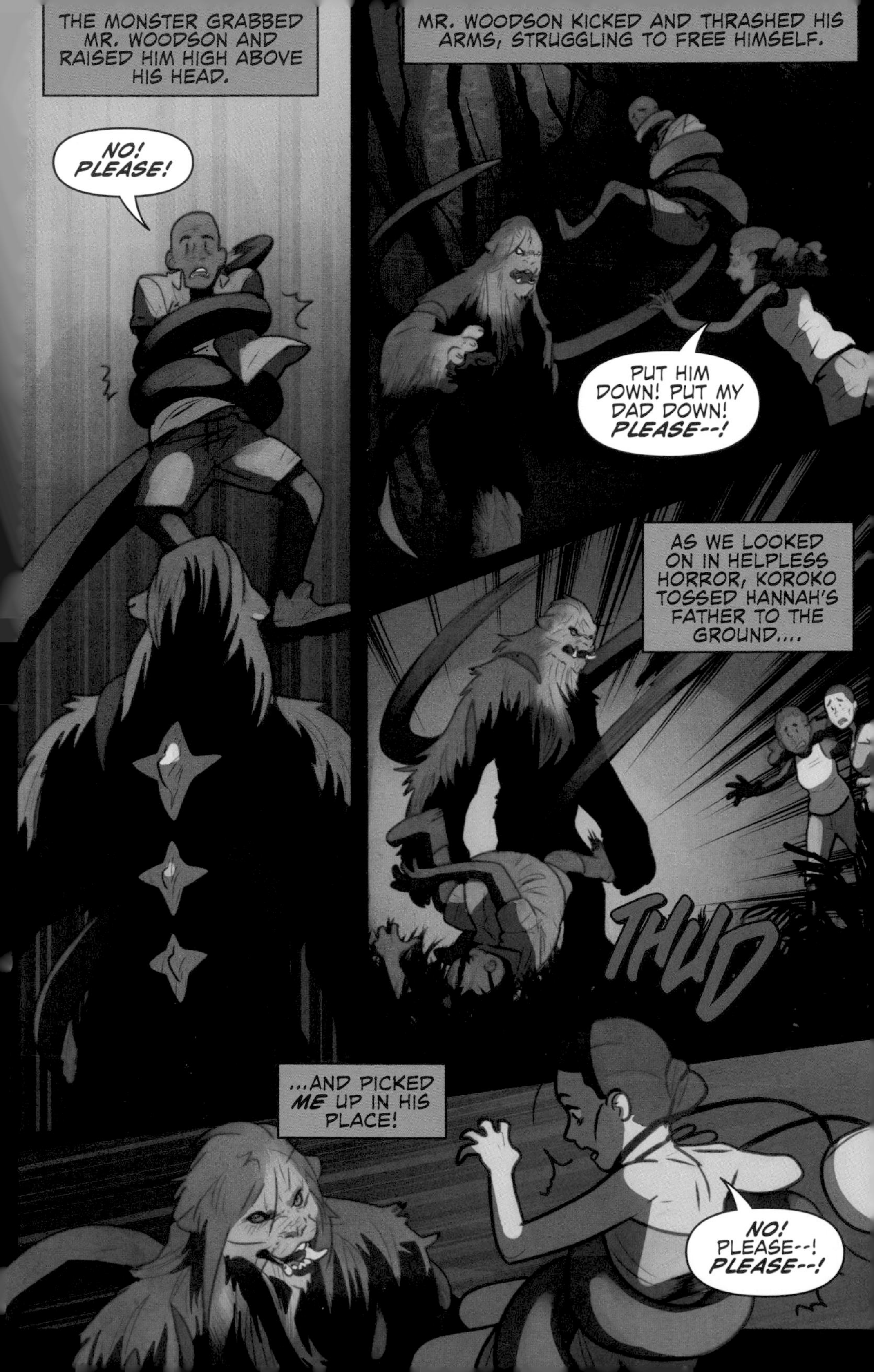
THE MONSTER GRABBED MR. WOODSON AND RAISED HIM HIGH ABOVE HIS HEAD.
NO! PLEASE!
MR. WOODSON KICKED AND THRASHED HIS ARMS, STRUGGLING TO FREE HIMSELF.
PUT HIM DOWN! PUT MY DAD DOWN! PLEASE--!
AS WE LOOKED ON IN HELPLESS HORROR, KOROKO TOSSED HANNAH'S FATHER TO THE GROUND....
THUD
...AND PICKED ME UP IN HIS PLACE!
NO! PLEASE--! PLEASE--!

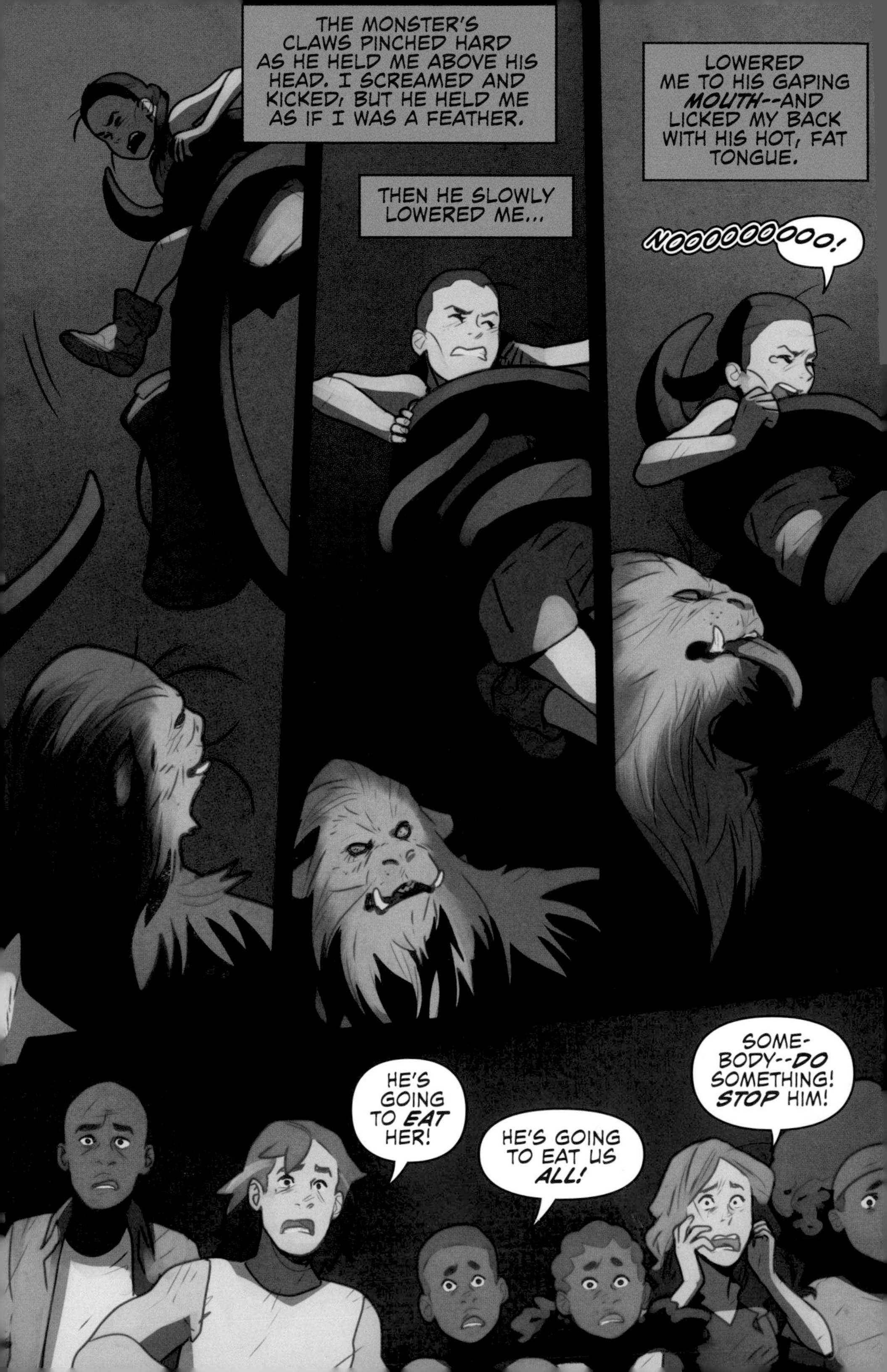
THE MONSTER'S CLAWS PINCHED HARD AS HE HELD ME ABOVE HIS HEAD. I SCREAMED AND KICKED, BUT HE HELD ME AS IF I WAS A FEATHER.
THEN HE SLOWLY LOWERED ME...
LOWERED ME TO HIS GAPING MOUTH--AND LICKED MY BACK WITH HIS HOT, FAT TONGUE.
NOOOOOOOOOO!
HE'S GOING TO EAT HER!
HE'S GOING TO EAT US ALL!
SOME-BODY--DO SOMETHING! STOP HIM!

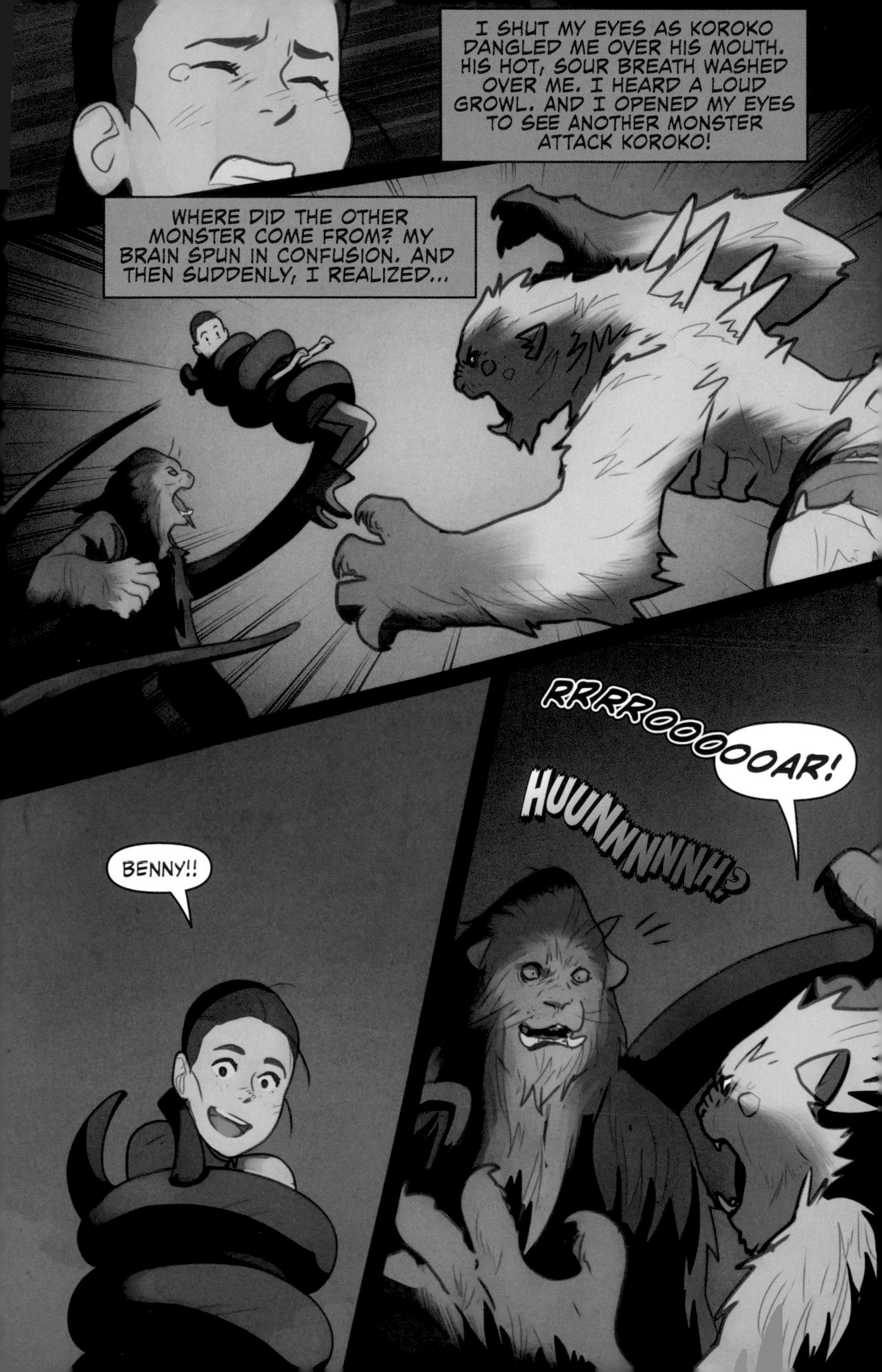
I SHUT MY EYES AS KOROKO DANGLED ME OVER HIS MOUTH. HIS HOT, SOUR BREATH WASHED OVER ME. I HEARD A LOUD GROWL. AND I OPENED MY EYES TO SEE ANOTHER MONSTER ATTACK KOROKO!
WHERE DID THE OTHER MONSTER COME FROM? MY BRAIN SPUN IN CONFUSION. AND THEN SUDDENLY, I REALIZED...
BENNY!!
RRRRROOOOOOAR!
HUUNNNNNNH?

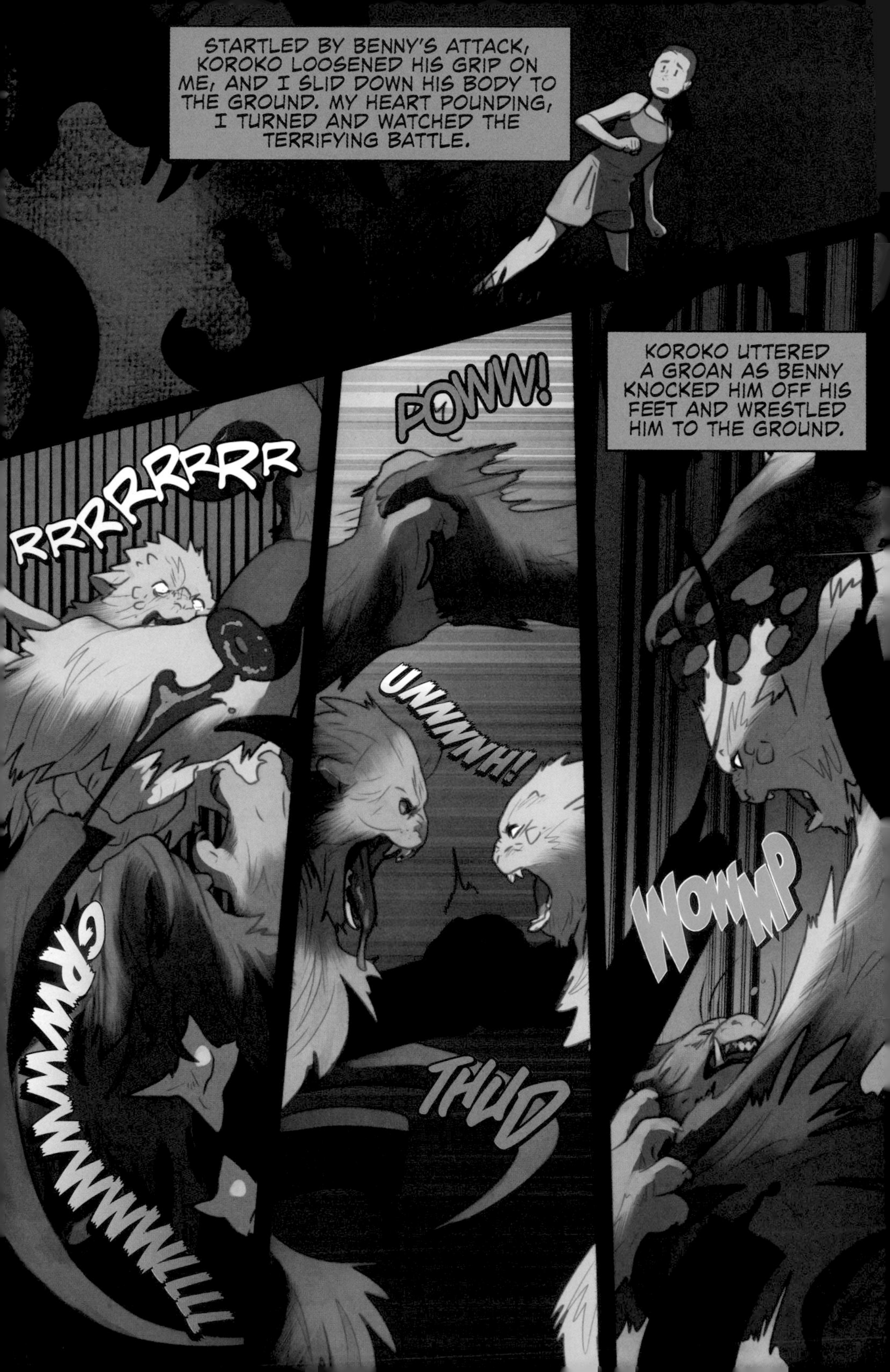
STARTLED BY BENNY'S ATTACK, KOROKO LOOSENED HIS GRIP ON ME, AND I SLID DOWN HIS BODY TO THE GROUND. MY HEART POUNDING, I TURNED AND WATCHED THE TERRIFYING BATTLE.
RRRRRRRRR
GRWWWWWWLLLL
POWW!
UNNNNNH!
THUD
KOROKO UTTERED A GROAN AS BENNY KNOCKED HIM OFF HIS FEET AND WRESTLED HIM TO THE GROUND.
WOMP

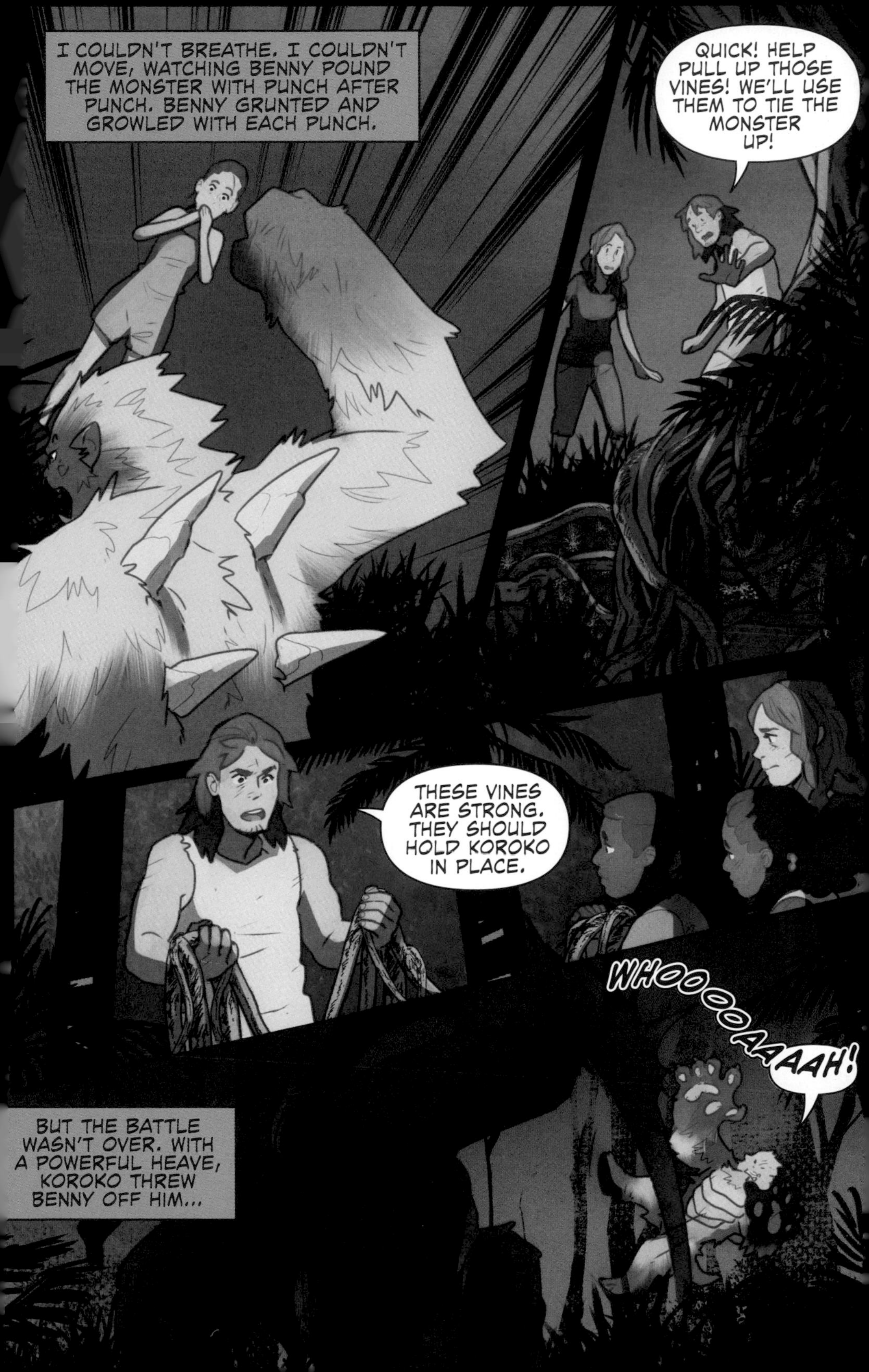
I COULDN'T BREATHE. I COULDN'T MOVE, WATCHING BENNY POUND THE MONSTER WITH PUNCH AFTER PUNCH. BENNY GRUNTED AND GROWLED WITH EACH PUNCH.
QUICK! HELP PULL UP THOSE VINES! WE'LL USE THEM TO TIE THE MONSTER UP!
THESE VINES ARE STRONG. THEY SHOULD HOLD KOROKO IN PLACE.
BUT THE BATTLE WASN'T OVER. WITH A POWERFUL HEAVE, KOROKO THREW BENNY OFF HIM...
WHOOOOOAAAAH!

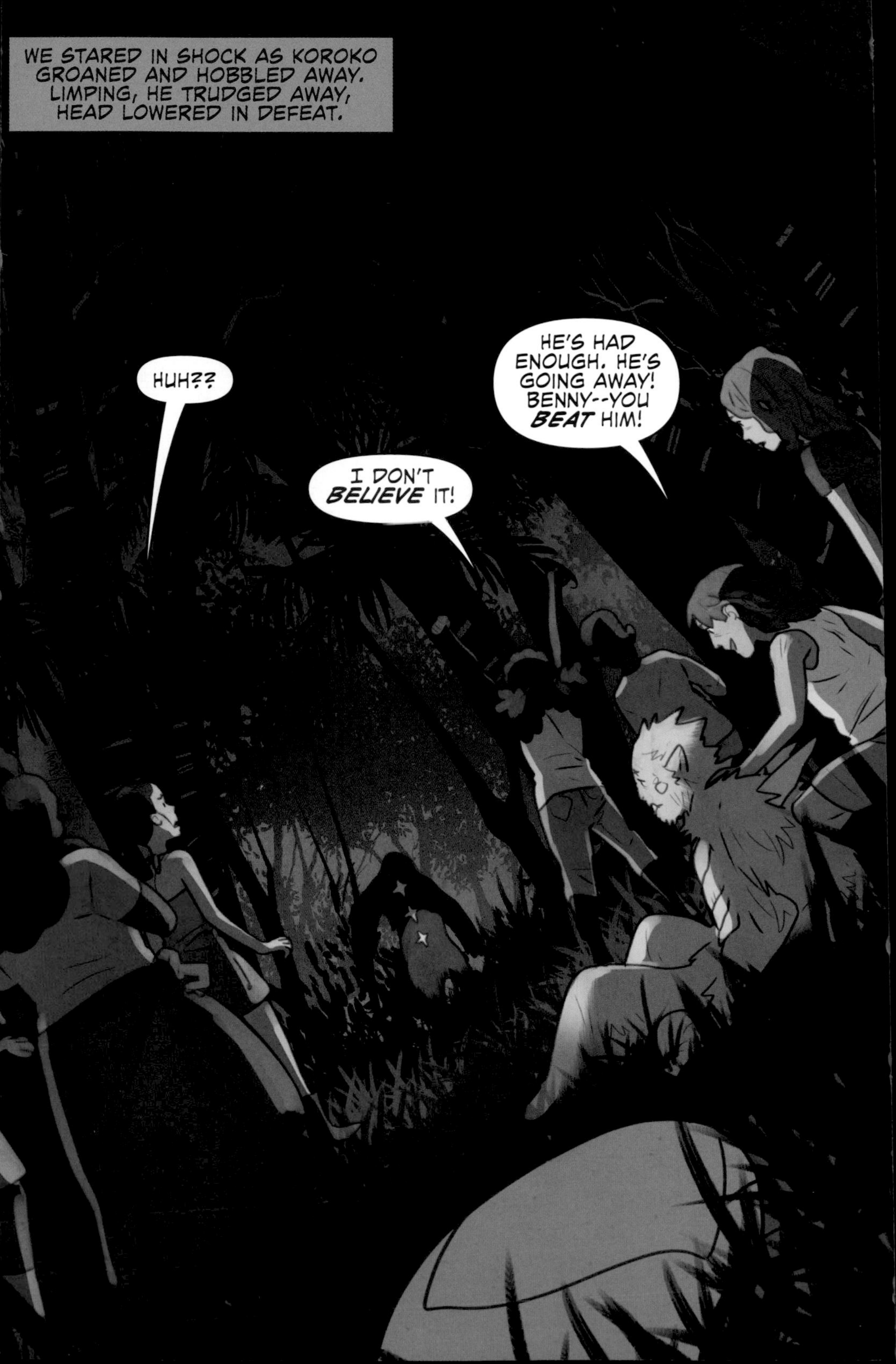
WE STARED IN SHOCK AS KOROKO GROANED AND HOBBLED AWAY. LIMPING, HE TRUDGED AWAY, HEAD LOWERED IN DEFEAT.
HUH??
I DON'T BELIEVE IT!
HE'S HAD ENOUGH. HE'S GOING AWAY! BENNY--YOU BEAT HIM!

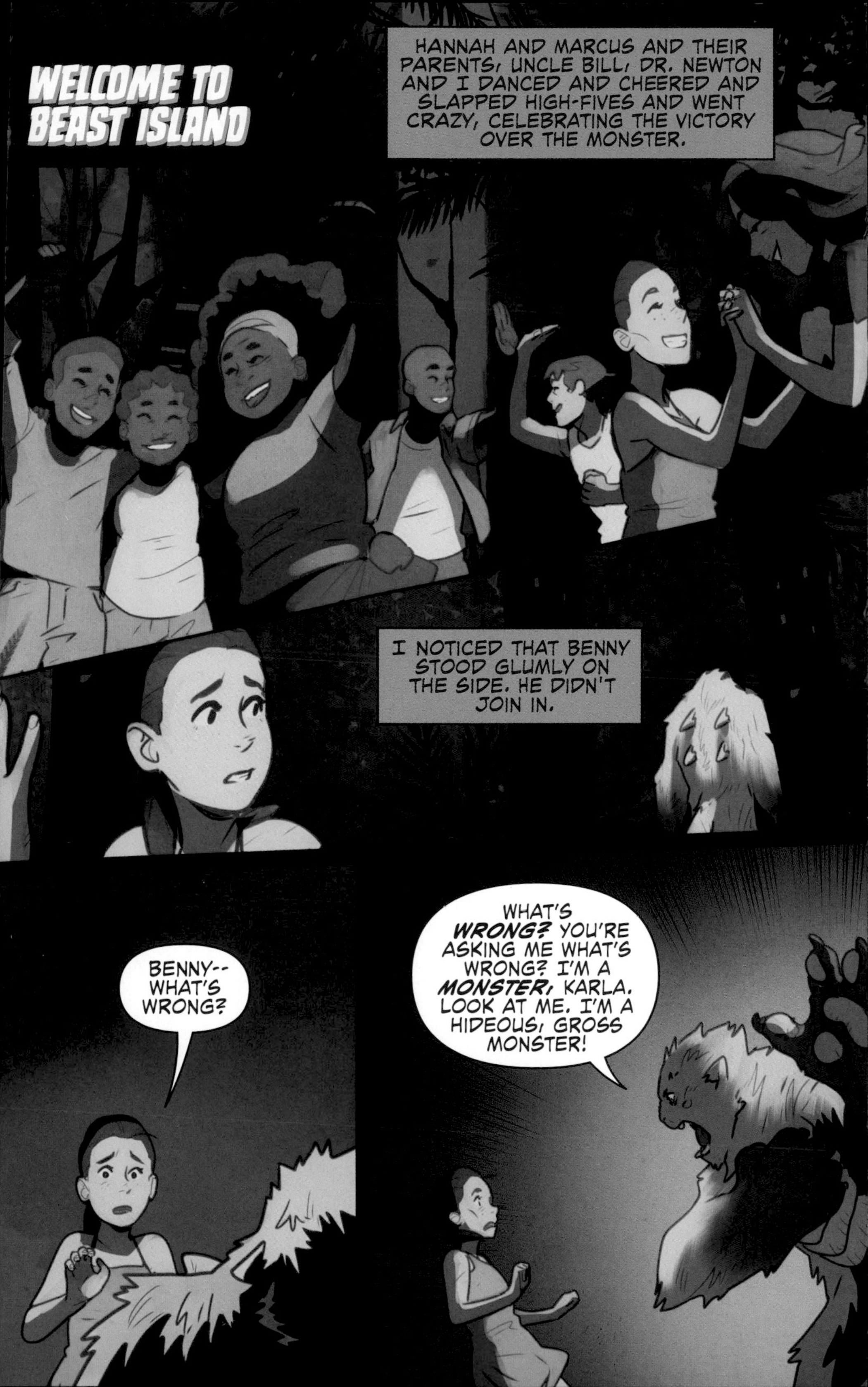
WELCOME TO BEAST ISLAND
HANNAH AND MARCUS AND THEIR PARENTS, UNCLE BILL, DR. NEWTON AND I DANCED AND CHEERED AND SLAPPED HIGH-FIVES AND WENT CRAZY, CELEBRATING THE VICTORY OVER THE MONSTER.
I NOTICED THAT BENNY STOOD GLUMLY ON THE SIDE. HE DIDN'T JOIN IN.
BENNY--WHAT'S WRONG?
WHAT'S WRONG? YOU'RE ASKING ME WHAT'S WRONG? I'M A MONSTER, KARLA. LOOK AT ME. I'M A HIDEOUS, GROSS MONSTER!

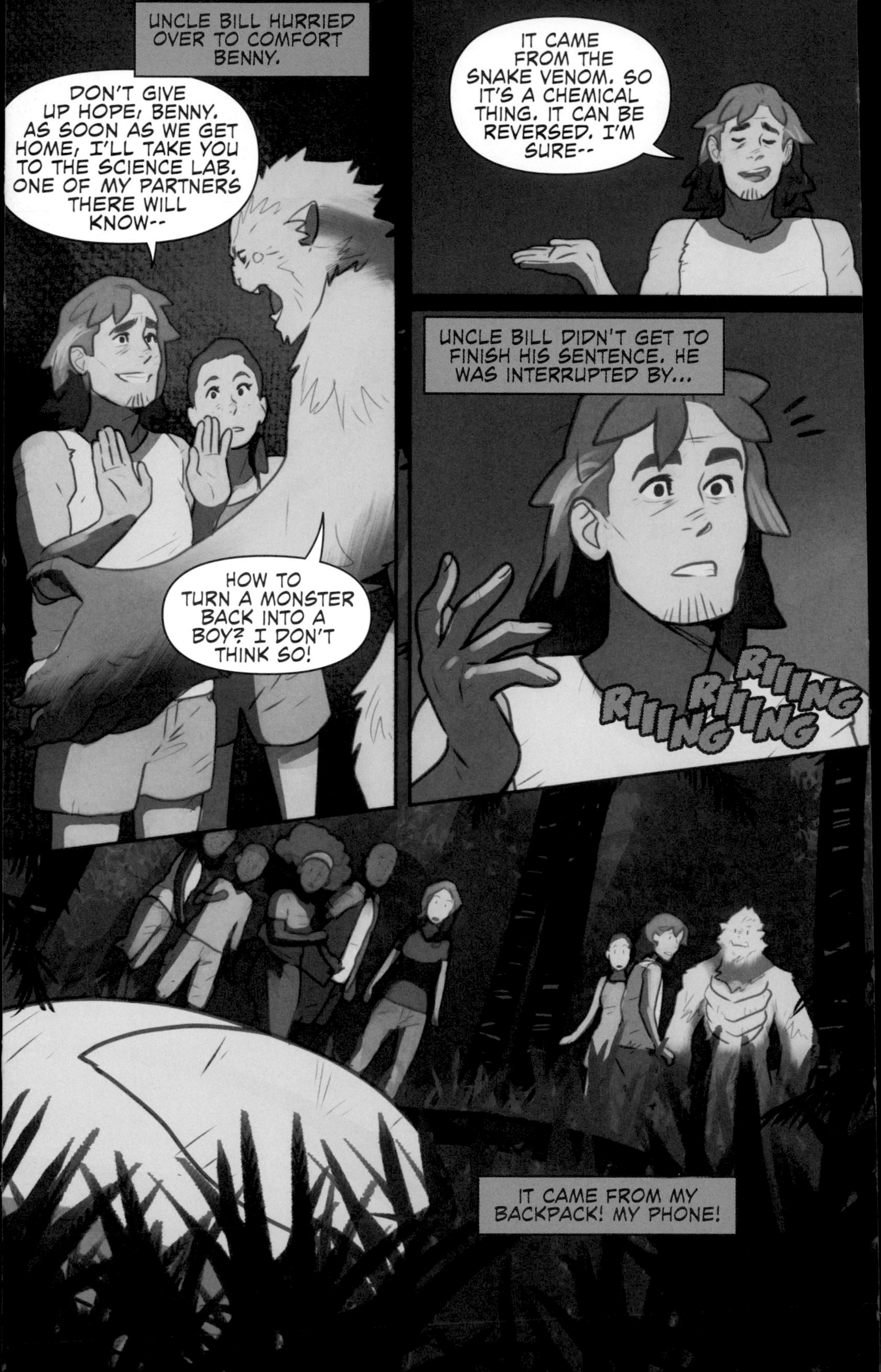
UNCLE BILL HURRIED OVER TO COMFORT BENNY.
DON'T GIVE UP HOPE, BENNY. AS SOON AS WE GET HOME, I'LL TAKE YOU TO THE SCIENCE LAB. ONE OF MY PARTNERS THERE WILL KNOW--
HOW TO TURN A MONSTER BACK INTO A BOY? I DON'T THINK SO!
IT CAME FROM THE SNAKE VENOM. SO IT'S A CHEMICAL THING. IT CAN BE REVERSED. I'M SURE--
UNCLE BILL DIDN'T GET TO FINISH HIS SENTENCE. HE WAS INTERRUPTED BY...
RIIING RIIING RIIING
IT CAME FROM MY BACKPACK! MY PHONE!

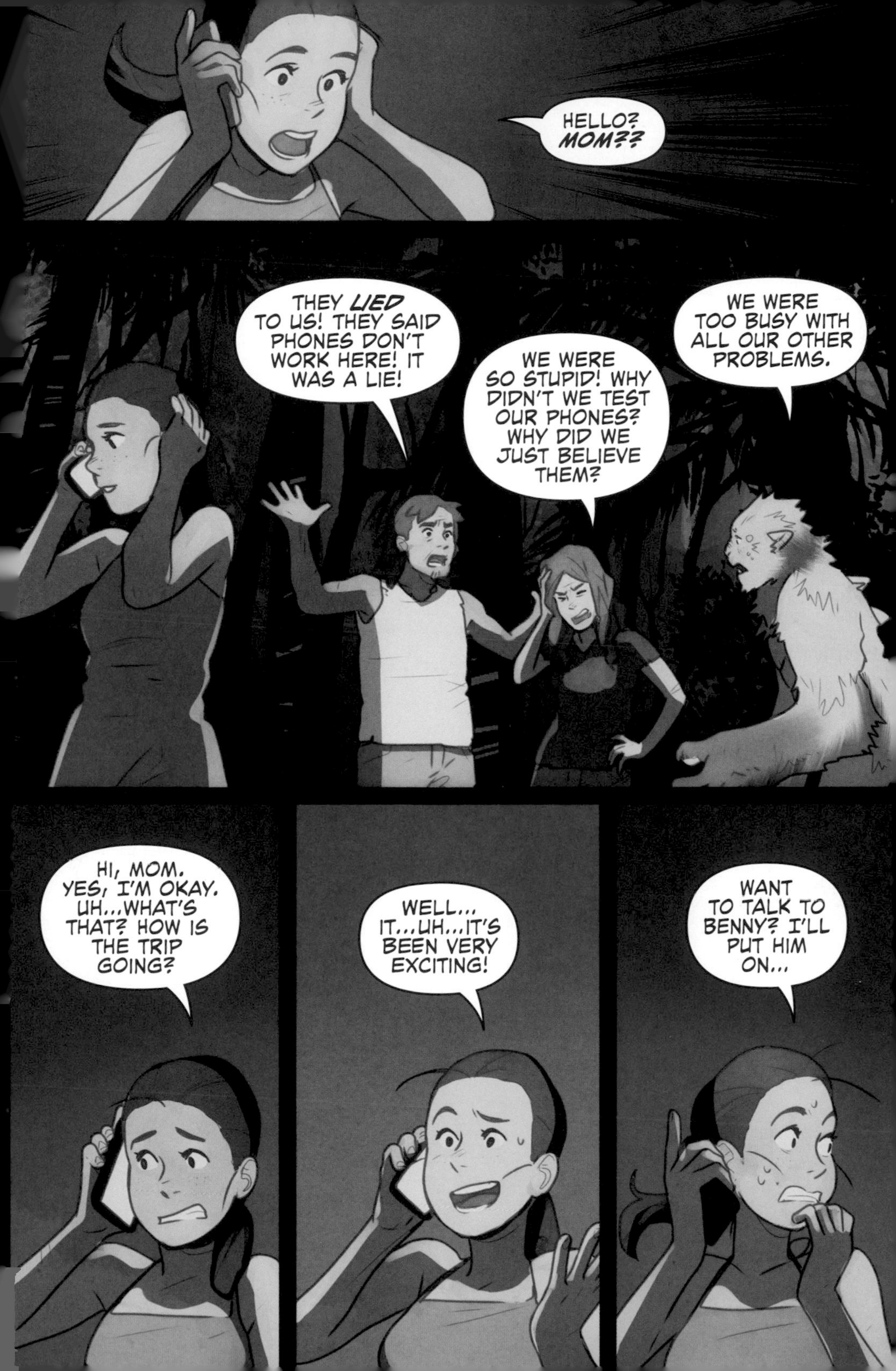
HELLO? MOM??
THEY LIED TO US! THEY SAID PHONES DON'T WORK HERE! IT WAS A LIE!
WE WERE SO STUPID! WHY DIDN'T WE TEST OUR PHONES? WHY DID WE JUST BELIEVE THEM?
WE WERE TOO BUSY WITH ALL OUR OTHER PROBLEMS.
HI, MOM. YES, I'M OKAY. UH...WHAT'S THAT? HOW IS THE TRIP GOING?
WELL... IT...UH...IT'S BEEN VERY EXCITING!
WANT TO TALK TO BENNY? I'LL PUT HIM ON...

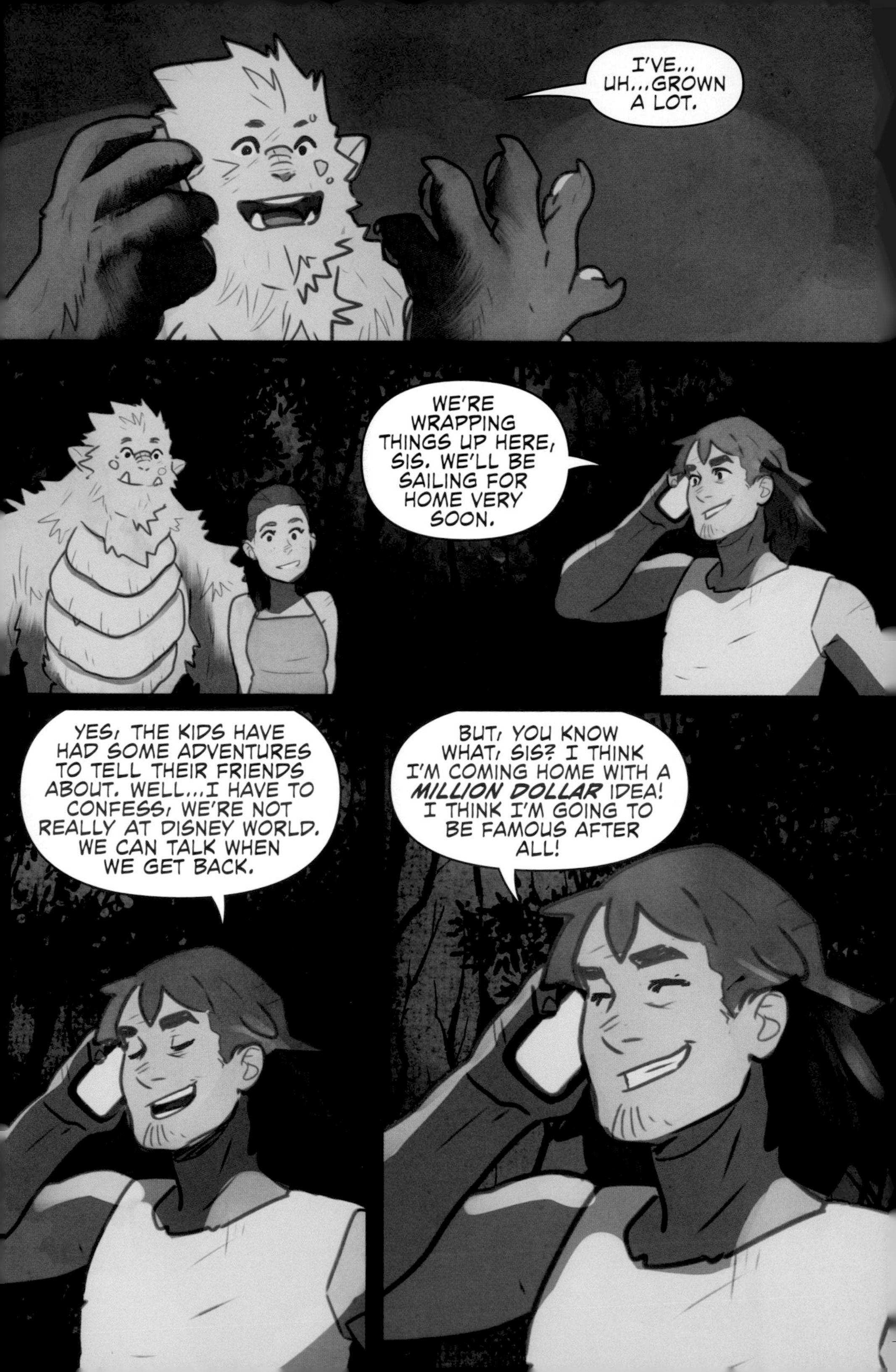
I'VE... UH...GROWN A LOT.
WE'RE WRAPPING THINGS UP HERE, SIS. WE'LL BE SAILING FOR HOME VERY SOON.
YES, THE KIDS HAVE HAD SOME ADVENTURES TO TELL THEIR FRIENDS ABOUT. WELL...I HAVE TO CONFESS, WE'RE NOT REALLY AT DISNEY WORLD. WE CAN TALK WHEN WE GET BACK.
BUT, YOU KNOW WHAT, SIS? I THINK I'M COMING HOME WITH A ***MILLION DOLLAR*** IDEA! I THINK I'M GOING TO BE FAMOUS AFTER ALL!

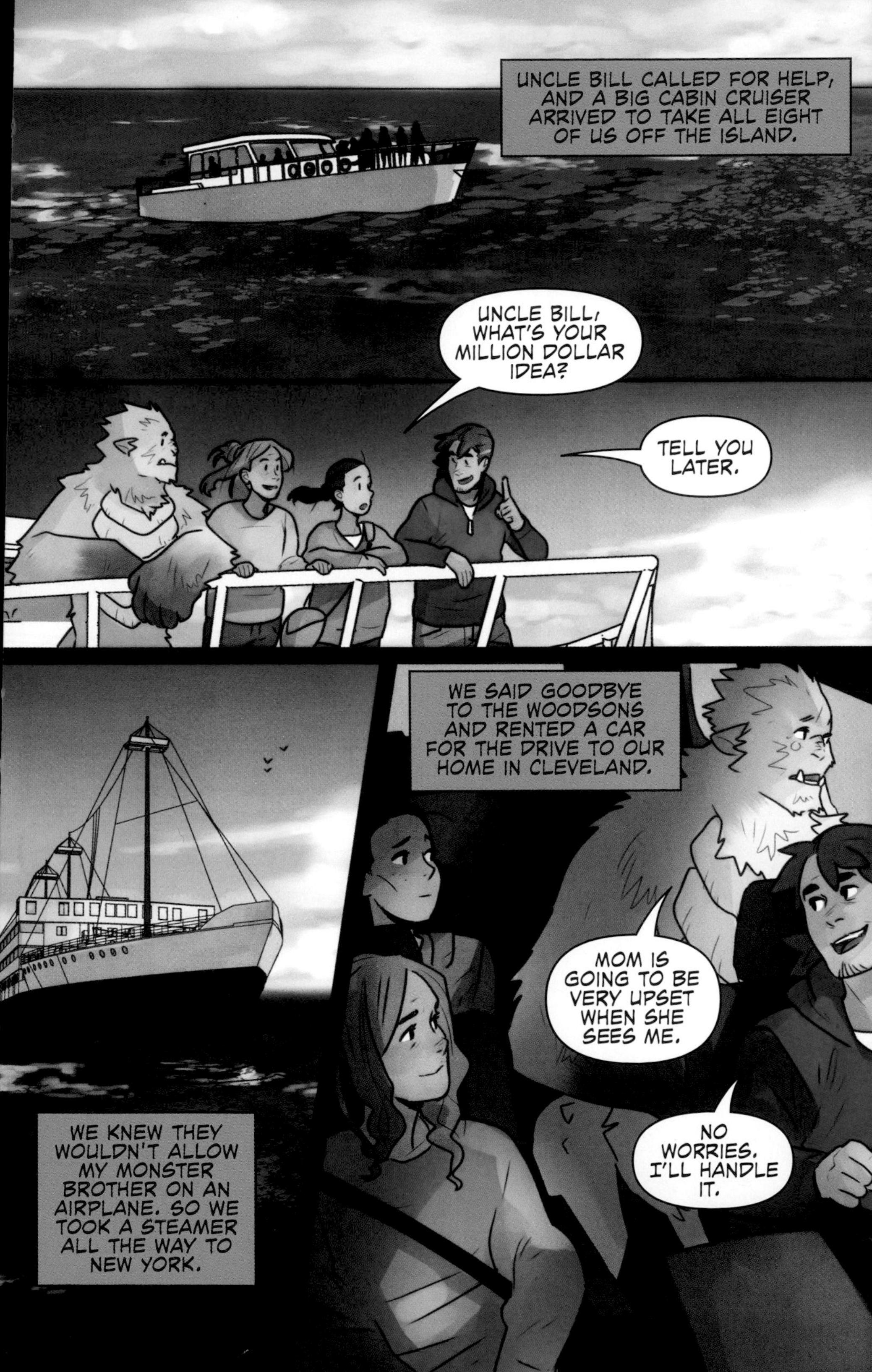
UNCLE BILL CALLED FOR HELP, AND A BIG CABIN CRUISER ARRIVED TO TAKE ALL EIGHT OF US OFF THE ISLAND.
UNCLE BILL, WHAT'S YOUR MILLION DOLLAR IDEA?
TELL YOU LATER.
WE KNEW THEY WOULDN'T ALLOW MY MONSTER BROTHER ON AN AIRPLANE. SO WE TOOK A STEAMER ALL THE WAY TO NEW YORK.
WE SAID GOODBYE TO THE WOODSONS AND RENTED A CAR FOR THE DRIVE TO OUR HOME IN CLEVELAND.
MOM IS GOING TO BE VERY UPSET WHEN SHE SEES ME.
NO WORRIES. I'LL HANDLE IT.

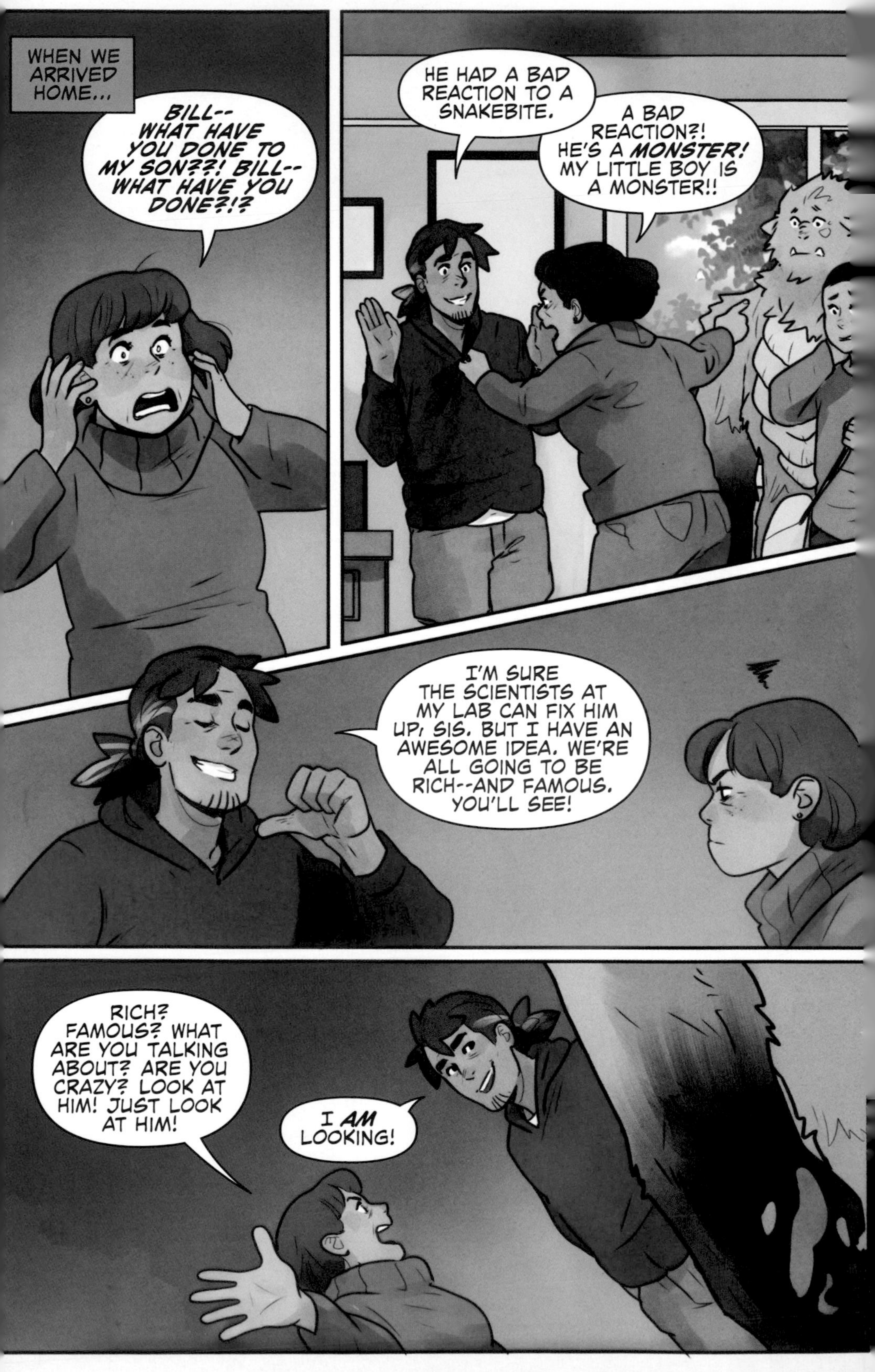
WHEN WE ARRIVED HOME...
BILL-- WHAT HAVE YOU DONE TO MY SON??! BILL-- WHAT HAVE YOU DONE?!?
HE HAD A BAD REACTION TO A SNAKEBITE.
A BAD REACTION?! HE'S A ***MONSTER!*** MY LITTLE BOY IS A MONSTER!!
I'M SURE THE SCIENTISTS AT MY LAB CAN FIX HIM UP, SIS. BUT I HAVE AN AWESOME IDEA. WE'RE ALL GOING TO BE RICH--AND FAMOUS. YOU'LL SEE!
RICH? FAMOUS? WHAT ARE YOU TALKING ABOUT? ARE YOU CRAZY? LOOK AT HIM! JUST LOOK AT HIM!
I ***AM*** LOOKING!

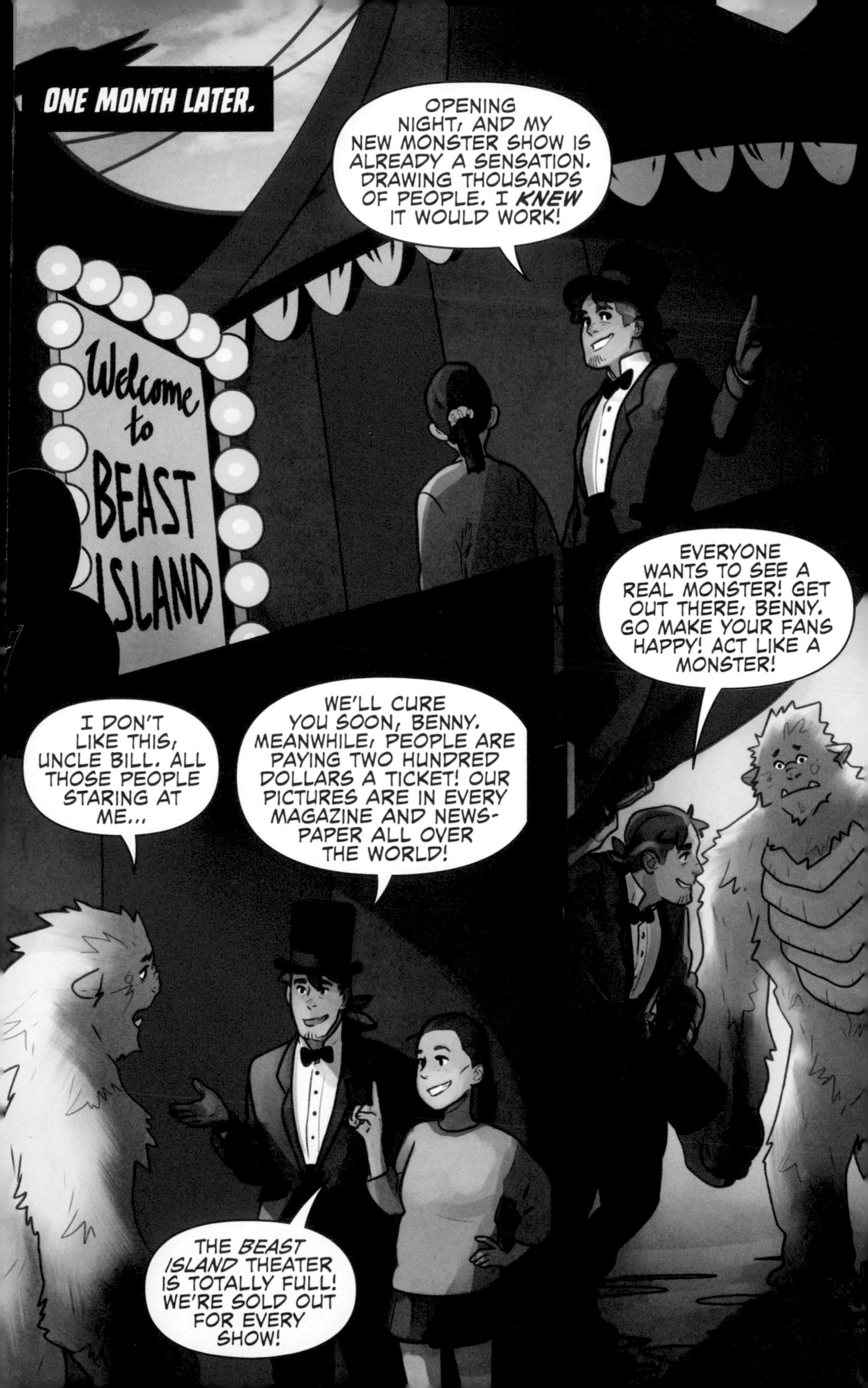
ONE MONTH LATER.
OPENING NIGHT, AND MY NEW MONSTER SHOW IS ALREADY A SENSATION. DRAWING THOUSANDS OF PEOPLE. I *KNEW* IT WOULD WORK!
Welcome to BEAST ISLAND
EVERYONE WANTS TO SEE A REAL MONSTER! GET OUT THERE, BENNY. GO MAKE YOUR FANS HAPPY! ACT LIKE A MONSTER!
I DON'T LIKE THIS, UNCLE BILL. ALL THOSE PEOPLE STARING AT ME...
WE'LL CURE YOU SOON, BENNY. MEANWHILE, PEOPLE ARE PAYING TWO HUNDRED DOLLARS A TICKET! OUR PICTURES ARE IN EVERY MAGAZINE AND NEWS-PAPER ALL OVER THE WORLD!
THE *BEAST ISLAND* THEATER IS TOTALLY FULL! WE'RE SOLD OUT FOR EVERY SHOW!

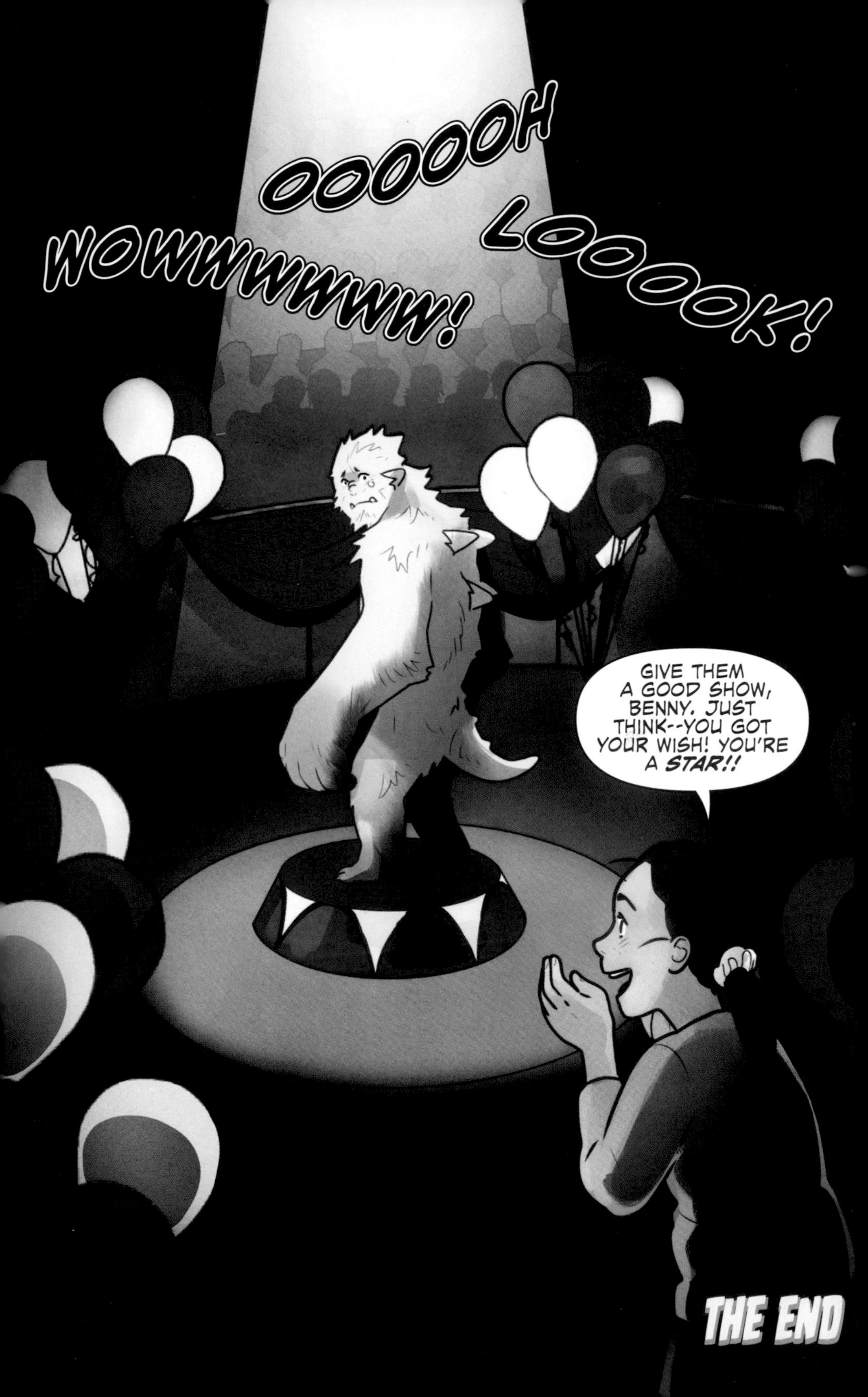
OOOOOOH
LOOOOOK!
WOWWWWWW!
GIVE THEM A GOOD SHOW, BENNY. JUST THINK--YOU GOT YOUR WISH! YOU'RE A *STAR!!*
THE END